good habits
intimacy
adulthood
guilt
boredom
entertainment
holiday
nature vs. nurture
rebellion
...escence
recognition
gravity
discretion
...ly
family values
...integrity
resignation
...ce
depression
midlife crisis
angst
commitment
divorce
freedom
meaning
...ome
whatever

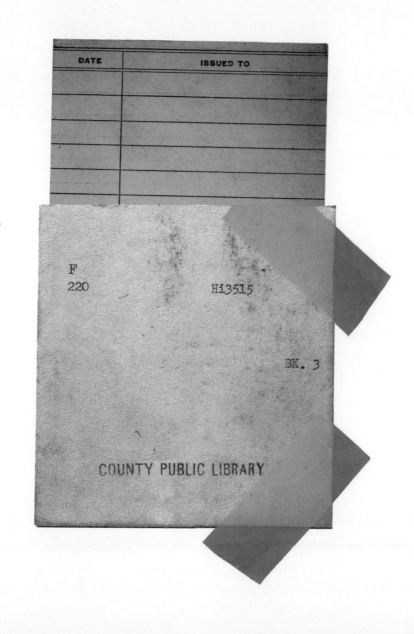

"A piece of the body torn out by the roots
might be more to the point."
                                    —Agee.

A FIELD GUIDE TO THE

❦

NORTH AMERICAN FAMILY

~A~
FIELD GUIDE
TO THE
NORTH AMERICAN
FAMILY

CONCERNING CHIEFLY THE HUNGATES AND HARRISONS; WITH
ACCOUNTS OF THEIR HABITS, NESTING, DISPERSION, ETC., AND
FULL DESCRIPTION OF THE PLUMAGE OF BOTH ADULT AND
YOUNG, WITHIN A TAXONOMIC SURVEY OF SEVERAL ASPECTS
OF FAMILIAL LIFE

BY

GARTH RISK HALLBERG
American Writer & Curator of afieldguide.com

WITH SIXTY-THREE ILLUSTRATIONS DONE BY VARIOUS ARTISTS.

Made by *Christopher D Salyers*,
with assistance from *Eliane Lazzaris*.

NEW YORK,
Published under the authority of Mark Batty Publisher.

FIRST EDITION
2007

TWO REPRESENTATIVE FAMILIES.

FRANK.

F. Harrison.

MARNIE.

M. Russo.

} LACEY, 1986.

THOMAS, 1987.

"Lying Tommy," "LT," "The Lieutenant."

JACK.

J. Hungate.

ELIZABETH.

E. Conroy.

} GABRIEL, 1986.

"Gabe."

JACQUELINE, 1995.

"Jackie."

HOW TO USE THIS BOOK.

The author sincerely hopes that this novella will prove to be of value for all readers. To that end, several methods have been provided for navigation.

A *capitalized guideword* appears at the top of each even-numbered page, denoting that page's entry. The reader may choose to move through the entries sequentially – which is to say, alphabetically.

Primary cross-references near the end of entries direct the reader to associated entries. The reader may wish to follow these cross-references until all entries have been read and the narrative is complete.

Secondary cross-references appear in Roman type within the italicized photo captions, and alert the curious reader to entries of interest. Like the primary cross-references, these may be used to move through the entries in a non-sequential fashion.

Some bold readers may even wish to peruse the book at random, or to consult the table of contents as need dictates. No matter; a narrative will eventually emerge.

The plates that adorn the volume are the work of the clever cameras of a number of artists, whose names and accomplishments are charted in the End Matter. Their illustrations will no doubt aid the understanding of those unfamiliar with the North American Family.

A Field Guide to the North American Family
© 2007 by Garth Risk Hallberg

All photographs © their respective photographers.

Design & production: Christopher D Salyers, Eliane Lazzaris
Editing: Buzz Poole

Typefaces used: Franklin Caslon; Synchro LET; and Fusaka Std

The author owes a debt of gratitude to Elise White; Buzz Poole, Mark Batty, Christopher D Salyers, John Paul Davis, and Jon Udelson; Matthew Elblonk and Nina Collins; Chris Eichler, Sai Sriskandarajah, Richard Bull, Janice Clark, and Jordan Alport; Jen Bekman and Tema Stauffer for taking a chance on the *Field Guide*; and all of the artists who generously contributed their time and talent.

Every effort has been made to trace accurate ownership of copyrighted text and visual materials used in this book. Errors or omissions will be corrected in subsequent editions, provided notification is sent to the publisher.

Library of Congress Control Number:
2007921479

Printed and bound in China

10 9 8 7 6 5 4 3 2 1   First edition

This edition © 2007
Mark Batty Publisher
36 West 37th Street, Penthouse
New York, NY 10018

www.markbattypublisher.com

ISBN-10: 0-9779850-9-1
ISBN-13: 978-09779850-9-8

Distributed outside North America by:

Thames & Hudson Ltd
181A High Holborn
London WC1V 7QX
United Kingdom
Tel: 00 44 20 7845 5000
Fax: 00 44 20 7845 5055
www.thameshudson.co.uk

FIELD GUIDE
ENTRIES

North Wal

N O

supposed Straits of Anian.

A M E

A
FIELD
GUIDE
TO THE
NORTH
AMERICAN
FAMILY

ADOLESCENCE

It's the boltcutters that open up a hole in the storm fence just big enough for a skinny boy to slip through. It's the backpack in which spraycans are rattling. One knows what one is doing, weaving back and forth among the dark hulks of traincars; it's the rails one must be careful to avoid. It's the memory of batteries blown up in earlier, smaller instances of life beyond the law. Or beyond the row of junked cars, the newer ones the mayor has pronounced paint-resistant. It's the rush of blood in the ears. The image on the backs of the eyes. It's the sky over the city sprayed violet, like the inside of one's heart – cloudy, brooding, suffused with dim glow after distant explosions.

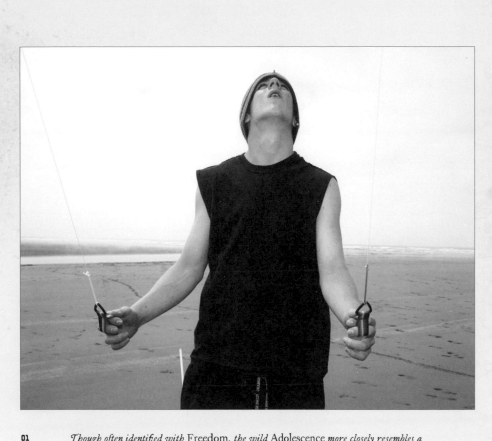

01   *Though often identified with* Freedom, *the wild* Adolescence *more closely resembles a*
Search for Meaning.

ADULTHOOD

Funerals weren't so different from elementary school. There were rules you learned sooner or later, the easy way or the hard way. Sit still. Listen. Offer your wife or daughter a hand to hold, as though holding hands was something your family still did. Squeeze to signify you might cry at what seem to be the appropriate moments. If you think you might actually cry, wear sunglasses. It was grim but true: like school and work and everything else in Jack Hungate's life, the funeral had eventually lost its novelty and become just another thing to plug into the day-planner, and by the end of his forties, he was averaging one or two every year: coworkers, fraternity brothers, relatives he'd forgotten he had. Neighbors. The sun was shining on the day they committed Frank Harrison to the earth, for example, and as Jack gazed through tinted lenses at the luminous blond hair on his own wife's and daughter's heads and at his son's nascent sideburns, he realized he'd never really known the man, despite having seen him at least once a week for the last decade – a total of hundreds of neighborly interactions. Several times each summer, Frank had brought his family over to barbecue and swim. Their kids were the same age, roughly. A memory floated up out of the haze: Frank Harrison emerging from the backyard pool, half-naked and hulking, his booming voice advertising his kingdom for a towel and a beer. And it dawned on Jack that it could just as easily have been his own blood vessels bursting. It could have been *his* heart. He struggled to remain somber. He looked out across the sea of stricken faces toward the faraway silver Sound. Incense was on the air. An eerie silence obtained, as after snowfall, broken only by the priest's litany and the drone of incoming planes and the widow's choked breathing. *It could have been me*, Jack thought, but it wasn't. A month later, when he and Elizabeth separated, he would find himself cursing the empty decorum of the country club set. But it served him well that day; no one could tell that inside he was rejoicing. Or that, although he ached for Marnie and the two Harrison kids, Lacey and whatshisname – Tommy – he'd never really cared for the dead man anyway.

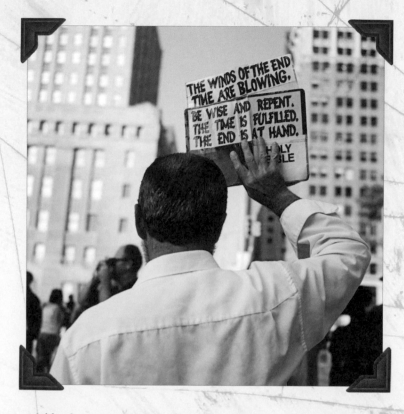

02 Adulthood *can be distinguished from* Maturity *by its tendency to cling to the chrysalis.*
On occasion, Adulthood *has even been known to disappear back into* Adolescence
following an unsettling foray out into the world.

SEE ALSO:
(032) DISCRETION   (034) DIVORCE   (042) FISCAL RESPONSIBILITY
(044) FREEDOM   (086) MIDLIFE CRISIS   (090) MORTGAGE
(118) SACRIFICE   (130) TRADITION

ANGST

⟿————⟾

Gabriel Hungate began to experiment at age 13, without the knowledge of his father or mother or younger sister. Described variously as "headstrong," "hard to peg," and "charismatic," he had long been an object of interest among the neighborhood males two to three years his senior. When in a local backyard one offered him a modified aluminum can and the remnants of a "dime-bag," he accepted immediately. It might just as easily have started with a Mini-Thin or a dose of Ritalin or a drink of tequila; in the blurred tumble of months that followed Gabriel speculated that, contrary to the rigid verticality of the "gateway hypothesis," stimulants and sedatives were networked horizontally, each linked to every other. Alcohol, nicotine, and cannabis, because the most readily available, were the intoxicants most often used among his cohort and by the subject himself. Typical symptoms of substance abuse (sullenness, academic underachievement, social withdrawal) were masked in Gabriel by a simultaneous upheaval in his domestic situation. His appetite for "downers" was well within the statistical mean for his sex and age; his tendencies to ingest in solitude and to keep the frequency and intensity of his intoxication secret even from his peers were outlier behaviors. Gabriel tended to conduct his experiments in his bedroom or the basement recreation room, and to further gauge his limits by playing music at high volume and sitting for hours in the dark in a state of self-recrimination. Even in the "kegger" setting, he drifted toward seclusion, where, he believed, anyone who cared to find him would come looking. No one came looking. Also notable, given the pattern of abuse over several years, was the abrupt cessation of these behaviors. Following the construction of a "graffiti wall" in the backyard of his mother's house, Gabriel Hungate, for reasons beyond the explanatory power of this study, gave up narcotics at an age (17) when most of his peers were intensifying their explorations. He began, instead, to paint (although, significantly, the patterns of withdrawal and self-reproach and heavy tobacco use would continue right up until his accident).

03   *The fossil record shows* Angst *to be a relative newcomer.* Possibly the product of
      crossbreeding between Boredom *and* Depression, Angst *made its first documented*
      appearance fewer than 500 years ago.

BOREDOM

Jackie roams the near-empty lower field with a handheld video camera, chasing the electrons in the broody grey air, the mist so fine it might be imaginary. Brake-lights stream beyond the chainlink fence. On the next field over, the varsity foot-ball team is practicing, and the war chants of teenagers puncture the pressurized quiet. A flock of greywhite birds is flushed from the hedge that separates the two fields. She chases them, her ponytail whipping around, her skirt and shirt too thin for the weather. She is narrating. "Today I lost a tooth." She captures the birds as they tumble in a dizzying fractal into the air, colors shifting light to dark. They gambol over a swimming pool that's been covered for winter and dwindle to dots in the sky. "They're running away. They don't like me," Jackie says. Trees scatter in the lens as she gallops away from the bushes. "The grass is brown." She spots a mudpuddle. "This is from when the trucks come across the field for a delivery." Now she lies down in the dry grass and aims the camera toward her face. "This is what it's like to be a bug. Not very exciting." She turns the camera around and positions her stuffed lion in front of the lens. It flops over. She reaches out to make an adjustment, but it flops again. An empty sandbox forms a backdrop. "This is Alphonse," she says. "Say hello, Alphonse. Hello! Behind him, that's the sandbox where I played at lunch today. I made a castle. Tomorrow I intend to play kickball. That's my video-journal for today. The end." The microphone drones dimly with white noise, and the camera continues to run, capturing the sandbox and the procession of blurred taillights far behind the flopped lion, whose mane is accreting fine raindrops. The voice cuts in again. "Oh, and also today, my parents got divorced. The end." The footage ends abruptly.

04

Once thought to be nonexistent where Entertainment *was present, this harmless parasite is now known to be present, to some degree, in every ecosystem.*

CHEMISTRY

Sugar. Sweet & Low. Caffeine to start the day. To unwind, alcohol: a beer or two, a glass of wine. Sherry or gin or a dry martini, by the chair by the pool, a glass or a bottle. Then Tylenol. Or for headaches, ibuprofen. For asthma, albuterol. Sniffles, sneezes, post-nasal drip: Robitussin, Nyquil, Dimetapp. The pantheon of name-brand pharmaceuticals, like poets of a dead tongue: Valium, Lithium, Xanex and Zoloft, Paxil and Prozac. Allegra, Viagra. Claritin, Clarinex, Retsin and Ritalin. The shelf in the medicine chest stuffed with Eli Lilly, GlaxoSmith-Kline, AstraZeneca. The horizons huffing opens up: gasoline, whipped cream, permanent markers, airplane glue and airbrush propellant. And then nicotine. Marijuana. Hashish. Opium. Amyl nitrates. Lysergic acid diethylamide. Psiolcy-bin. Mescaline. Methamphetamines and amphetamines. Cocaine to kill pain. No different than a Codeine pill. No different than Demerol, or Percoset. The baby aspirin doctors recommend most. The epidural, even before the birth.

05   Chemistry *is a species of the phylum* Entertainment.

COMMITMENT

At first the black lady behind the desk said visiting hours were over. I could understand where she was coming from – she could have lost her job over breaking hospital regulations – so I tried to keep smiling, because I didn't want her to feel bad about what was, after all, just doing her job. But like my dad used to say back when he was still alive, I have a lousy poker face, and after a few seconds, she sighed. "All right. Tell me what's going on." Her face was businesslike, but her eyes were kind, I noticed. And it just started spilling out of me, about cheerleading running over and Tommy being late with the car and how it would be so hard for me to get across town to the hospital by eight on Tuesdays and Thursdays to see my boyfriend, the patient. She asked his name and I told her, Gabriel. Gabriel Hungate. She found his chart and studied it for a minute. "Like the archangel," I said. Then she told me that she was in charge on weeknights and, so long as I didn't tell anyone, she'd take me back to see him whenever I could get there. That's how I started going every night to the burn unit. It was kind of nice, actually, after all the visitors were gone, even his family, and it could be just him and me. I could talk to him and read to him and sometimes just sit quietly with my hand resting on his one unbandaged hand and try to feel him talking to me through his skin. I could cry and no one would know. That's another thing my dad had told me: I led a charmed life, everything would always work out for me. His voice was staticky when he said it; we must have had a bad connection. And on Christmas Eve morning I made sugar cookies from scratch. It started snowing as I drove over to the hospital to leave them at the front desk for the heavyset nurse who had bent the rules for me. It turned out she was on vacation. Still, I left them for whoever was scheduled to work that night.

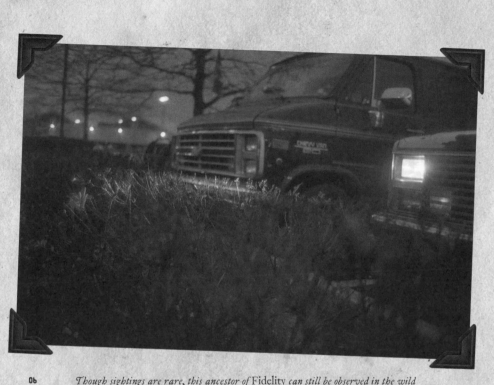

06 *Though sightings are rare, this ancestor of* Fidelity *can still be observed in the wild today.*

CONSENSUS

We can all agree on this much, Marnie thought: nobody saw the Hungate divorce coming. Of course she'd heard through her daughter that Jack and Elizabeth had been having some difficulties, but what couple didn't? Lord knows Frank had sometimes gone for months without touching her and had sometimes worked late and had sometimes retreated to his study with his *Wall Street Journal* without so much as asking about anyone else's day. But at those times, Marnie had looked to the Hungates. In the privacy of her own mind, she saw them as the last of a dying breed, the Great American Family. She'd actually found herself wondering: WWED? What Would Elizabeth Do? Other times, she even felt a little jealous of her slender, blonde neighbor with her sensitive husband and her popular son and her still-small daughter and her big, kidney-shaped swimming pool. It was by that swimming pool, in fact, on the first warm day after Frank died, that Marnie found herself eyeing a knife as Elizabeth lounged nearby in a two-piece, not really listening to the answers to her questions. But Marnie had had years of experience smiling and swallowing, and she reminded herself that some people had all the luck. It wasn't anyone's fault, that's just the way it was. So she was shocked when Lacey announced at breakfast a few weeks later that Gabe's parents were separating. No one at the Friends of the Library cookout could agree on what caused it. Some people insinuated that Jack Hungate was having an affair, but personally, Marnie didn't buy it. Jack had always been a stand-up guy, and she didn't approve of scuttlebutt. Nonetheless, she found herself wanting to know more about the divorce, and every time the subject came up she felt a little flutter of something like gratitude, for which on Sundays she always confessed.

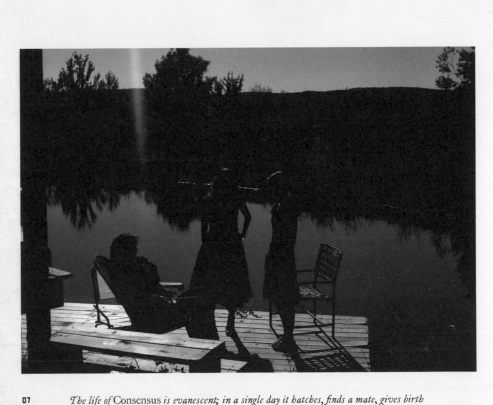

07   *The life of* Consensus *is evanescent; in a single day it hatches, finds a mate, gives birth and dies.*

CUSTODY BATTLE

When your house is never clean enough. When your food is never healthy enough. When you're perpetually five to fifteen minutes late to meet them in the parking lot of Ken's Big Boy, the neutral zone where your estranged wife insists you meet to exchange your daughter on Wednesdays and alternating weekends. Her Volvo, formerly yours, will be waiting, the sun on the windshield obscuring the passengers within. She always leaves the engine running these days, as if to underscore the point: you're not on time, and she has places to be. Your daughter will adopt these grievances as her own, but they will retain the familiar tang of Elizabeth, like the pillowcase that still smells of her shampoo. Like the photos in the yearbooks you left behind when you moved out.

08   *Descended from* Divorce, Custody Battle *is one of several natural predators of the* Amicable Parting.

SEE ALSO:
(050) GRIEF   (066) INFIDELITY   (100) PHASE
(112) RECONCILIATION   (118) SACRIFICE   (130) TRADITION

DEPRESSION

Instant oatmeal for breakfast. It was always instant oatmeal in the winter. I had grown bored with the available flavors: Maple & Brown Sugar, Apples & Cinnamon, Raisins & Spice. Once, there had been a Cinnamon & Spice, but now you had to make your own by excavating all the raisins, moving them to one side of the bowl. I used the convex part of the spoon to smooth out little trenches in the surface of the oatmeal and then watched as they filled up with milk. "Aren't you hungry, Tommy?" my mom wanted to know. She was packing lunches on the other side of the kitchen island. I told her my stomach hurt, which was partially true, in that it would hurt by the time I got to school if I didn't eat something. "You look tired," she said. The milk wasn't filling the trenches fast enough. I hacked out deep crevasses with the end of the spoon. I rolled the raisins in and covered them over. I told her I had been up late doing homework. Really, I had been lying under the covers naked and stoned, listening to the noises that meant my sister and Gabe were dry-humping instead of studying in the next room, or rather the lack of noise, the silence that seeped through the sheetrock walls and the pillow. Wondering if Gabe had felt this way back when he was using. Sometimes at school I said things that maybe were a little exaggerated to appear more interesting, but I usually tried to be honest with my mom. It was just that with my dad gone, there were certain things I couldn't tell her. I couldn't tell her, for example, that half the kids last year had thought I was making it up about Dad until Lacey confirmed the reason we'd been absent for a week. I couldn't tell her that I couldn't sleep anymore unless I masturbated beforehand. And I couldn't tell her that this fucking breakfast made me want to puke. I pretended to take a couple bites and then, when her back was turned, got up and dumped the bowl down the garbage disposal. I pulled on my backpack full of stolen compact discs and graphing calculators and pecked her on the cheek and breezed out the front door, trying to give the impression that, on this day like every other, there was anything to look forward to.

Having evolved from a ruminant species known as Melancholia, Depression *now dominates the animal kingdom. Its explosive growth curve remains unaccounted for, but some Family-watchers have pointed to a concurrent surge in* Search for Meaning.

SEE ALSO:
(014) ADOLESCENCE   (016) ADULTHOOD

DISCRETION

She would never say who, and there were times when Jack wondered whether knowing his identity would have made it better or worse – afternoons that first fall when he sat on the back porch with a can of beer and a cigarette, ready to hide the latter at the first hint of a car pulling into the drive. False alarms were constant. He would stub out a Marlboro halfway through, only to gather from the unbroken silence of the house behind him that the engine-whine he'd heard heralded the arrival of one of his new neighbors, and not his son. He'd given Gabe a little used Geo for his birthday back in September, when he and Elizabeth were still wavering about the separation, like the two last leaves on a branch (as though there were anything to do but give in to gravity). Now he wondered if this wasn't part of what kept Gabe coming back, some obscure sense of obligation. Certainly Jackie had added the car to an already formidable dossier of evidence that her father favored his firstborn. The aroma of tobacco that hovered around Gabe when he appeared in the afternoons after school made Jack pretty sure that his son was secretly a smoker, too. But what could he say? Besides, it almost made him feel closer to the boy. And perhaps Gabe made the crosstown trip so often (far more than the custody agreement stipulated) just to have an excuse to be in the car alone, where he could smoke in private. Jackie never visited anymore. In this way and in most others, she and her brother offset each other. Jack scanned the new backyard. Maybe he would build a wall here that Gabe could paint on, as Elizabeth had reportedly done. The sky, hemmed in by the evergreens at the edges of the backyard, was grey, and had been for weeks. The grass was getting crispy. The wind that gusted up and rattled the windchimes was nothing like it used to be, off the bay. At the old house, he couldn't have gotten the cigarette lit. He decided he would have felt better knowing if it had been Martin Luther King and worse if it had been Jack Kennedy. Better if it was Eric Clapton and worse if it was Peter Frampton. Better knowing if it was over. Worse if it was still going on. Better knowing if it was a complete stranger. Otherwise, better to remain in the dark.

N.B.: Discretion *and* Privacy *are not the same animal.*

DIVORCE

He knew, oh, he knew, he saw it coming, he kept asking her, while she gardened, while she unloaded the dishwasher, while she flipped again through the takeout menus unable to find what she wanted, are you happy, Mom, are you happy, knowing somehow she wasn't, and no, the knowing didn't make it any better, because another thing he knew, like he knew his own face in the mirror, was that it was his fault, because what was Mom doing, sitting in the corner of the living room with the headphones on every night that week, if not taking a cue from her son...if not, herself, withdrawing? He heard folk music sloshing out of the earphones like water over the rim of a bowl. He had half a mind to go through Mom's underwear drawer, to see if she, too, had a stash. Then Dad, on the couch with a stack of papers, was asking her a question that she, in her earphones, couldn't hear, and asking again, louder. And then both voices were raised, as Gabe had known they would be – something was happening, as he had known it would – and he went to the basement with the lights off and took the last two pills from the film-canister in his pocket and swallowed them without water and knelt in the middle of the rug, and he swore it would be the last time, but oh, he knew, he had done it, he had done it now.

11   *Due to a growth curve similar to that of* Depression, *a robust* Divorce *population has become common wherever* Love *dwells in large numbers.*

ENTERTAINMENT

In the beginning was the Television. And the Television was large and paneled in plastic made to look like wood. It dwelled in a dim corner of the living room and came on for national news, *Cosby*, Saturday cartoons, Sunday football and little else. And man and woman huddled close to one another on the sofa or stretched out on the rug, and it was good. When man made partner, they bought a VCR, and soon afterwards another Television, this one sleeker but less modest. And they began to watch videos together in the darkness, and there was popcorn. In the fifth year, the cable company created a premium-channel package. And it was affordable. And woman had moved up in the mayor's office. And so they said why not. After days of toil, to sit and feast in front of the Television, and not to have to think of something to say, was for man and woman a kind of heaven. And then Nintendo said: let there be Duck Hunt. Let there be Mario Brothers. Let there be Nintendo 64 and GameCube. And the children saw that these were good, though it was not possible to watch and play at once. Thus was there purchased a children's Television, and unto it was given its own room, the furnished basement. And it came to be a refuge for daughter and son when the silence upstairs ended and the fighting began. Where once they had sat together squabbling over the controllers, they now took turns occupying the room alone, turning up the sound to drown out the voices through the floorboards. And save for the screen's blue light, darkness was on the faces of the children.

12   *With its rapid mutation rate,* Entertainment *adapts readily to changes in the environment. Easily housebroken, it is welcomed in most North American Homes.*

SEE ALSO:
(020) BOREDOM   (022) CHEMISTRY   (054) HABITS, BAD
(074) IRONY   (078) MATERIAL   (102) PRIVACY
(124) SIBLING RIVALRY   (136) WHATEVER

FAMILY VALUES

Long after his life ceased to resemble the one he'd imagined for himself as a kid
– after crisp slacks replaced bluejeans, a house on Long Island replaced the East
Side walkup, and the rush of short-selling a future replaced that of blowing a
line and he ceased to recognize the Brooklyn girl he'd bedded in the overweight
homemaker he'd married – Frank listened to The Who. He kept disc three of the
boxed set in the Suburban at all times and disc four in his Discman. The world
around him no longer struck power chords, but stranded in rush-hour traffic or
lifting weights at his financial district gym, he could still feel locked inside his ribs
the hunger that had found its perfect expression in "The Seeker," in "Won't Get
Fooled Again." Even when there was no music, The Who played in his head. It
was "Who Are You" that he was hearing this afternoon, in the Hungates' backyard. He was standing with Jack next to the grill, ostensibly absorbing the details
of some legal case, but all that was in his head was "Who are you? Who, who,
who, who?" He took a drag of his cigarette and looked over at the pool. Tommy
was standing in the shallow end, a wet white tee-shirt clinging to his flabby boy-
breasts. He was sticking his tongue out at the little Hungate girl, Jackie, who was
sticking her tongue out at him. Tommy's tongue disappeared when Elizabeth
knelt down at the edge of the water to ask him if he wanted a Coke. She wore a
tee-shirt over her bikini top; her tanned legs folded sinuously beneath her. Frank
felt a stirring beneath his swim trunks...and then embarrassment as the boy said,
"Yeah." "How about a thank-you?" Frank called to him. "That's my boy," he
added, after his flushed son had stammered out his gratitude; he didn't want her
to think that they weren't close, he and Tommy, or that he wasn't the kind and
caring father he in point of fact was. And before rising to disappear into the house,
she rewarded him with a brief smile. He apologized to Jack. "We just really
emphasize respect in our house. You were saying?" Out of guilt for his impure
thoughts, he worked extra-hard to give the illusion that he was listening, but the
Roger Daltrey in his head kept screaming, "Who the fuck are you?"

13   *Specimens of this type – a toy breed of* Tradition *– are recognizable by their seeming delicacy and attractive plumage. Be careful handling* Family Values, *however: beneath their camouflage lies a perpetual and undomesticated carnality.*

FIDELITY

———

Like that time? The time we totally knew but were afraid to tell you that that boyfriend of yours was messing around with your former supposed friend Michelle, who we can now all agree is a total bitch and who sometimes we secretly think would have been a match made in heaven for Gabe in terms of being way selfish and also spacey if what happened hadn't happened, and he was probably like tattooing swans on her forearms with a ballpoint pen or something the way he did to win you over? That whole time if you would have just brought your concerns to us we would have known you wouldn't be totally shattered to learn the truth. Because, I mean, we were always looking out for you, girl, that's what you do when you care. For example when he got third-degree burns over eighty percent of his body. Because after that that skank washed her hands of him, but you, you were able to forgive, maybe because there was more to him than we knew but probably more because you're pretty much incapable of cruelty.

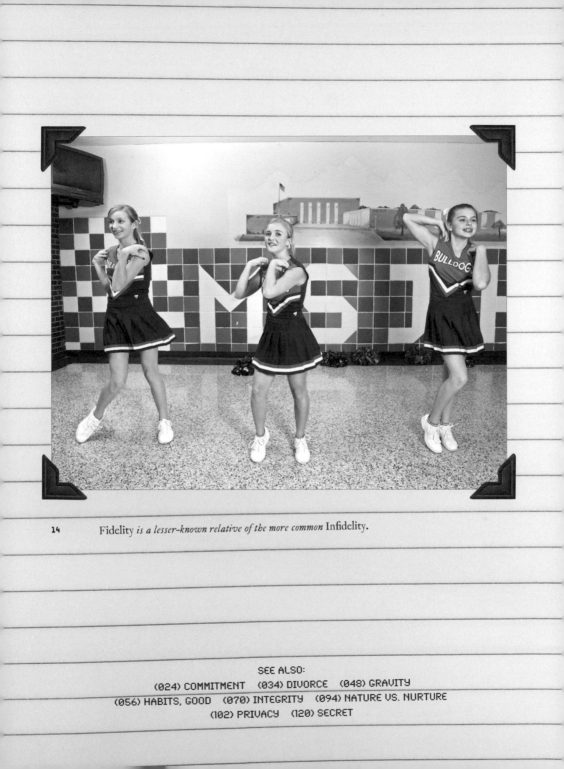

14   Fidelity *is a lesser-known relative of the more common* Infidelity.

FISCAL RESPONSIBILITY

Not to put too fine a point on it, Mr. and Ms. Big-Time GOPAC contributor, but the private sector ain't going to offer to pick up the tab when, after a gruesome accident and a three-month hospital stay, your son's medical bills pass the million-dollar mark. Although, on second thought, it will employ the doctor who will wield the scalpel during the skin grafts, so maybe it's all right after all. And think of all the magazines you'll read in the waiting room! The sweet efflorescence of the media conglomerates! Think of the market-driven advances in chair design! The commercials on the television in the corner! Now, all in all, aren't you feeling pretty good about the private sector?

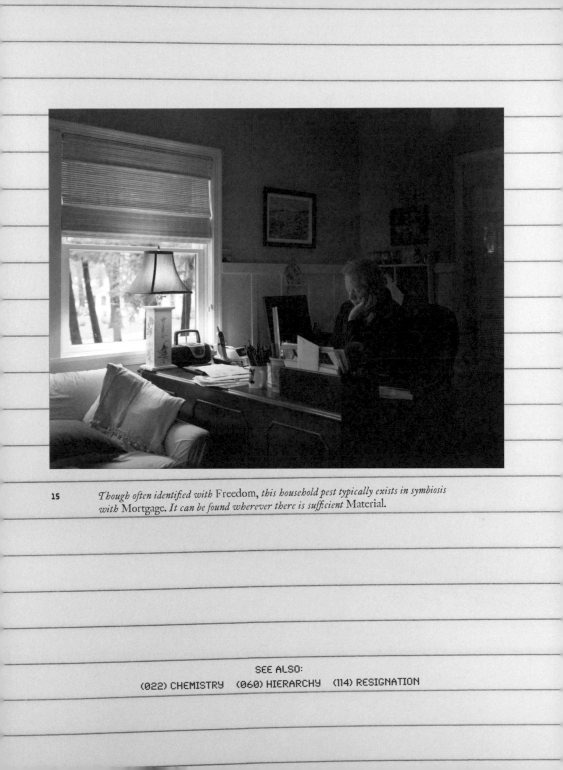

15   *Though often identified with* Freedom, *this household pest typically exists in symbiosis with* Mortgage. *It can be found wherever there is sufficient* Material.

SEE ALSO:

(022) CHEMISTRY   (060) HIERARCHY   (114) RESIGNATION

FREEDOM

Elizabeth's been working out. Kicking along with her tae bo video. Listening to mid-period Joni Mitchell while she runs in front of the big picture window on a treadmill rescued from the obscurity of the garage. Reading Susan Faludi and Anaïs Nin. Country line-dancing and wearing tall boots and eating ice cream for lunch. She's been doing things she never would have when she was married to Jack. She's been doing things because she never would have when she was married to Jack. She's constantly aware of all that's broken or lost: the trust of her son, the happiness of her daughter, the comforting warm lump of a husband in the bed beside her, the narrative of her life, but she's been telling herself it was worth it. And on a country road north of Westchester one day, edging the Volvo's speedometer toward 90 miles per hour, just because she can, she wonders, does this count as liberation?

1b *Perhaps because of its resemblance to the endangered* Meaning, Freedom *is the single most sought-after creature in North America. Like* Entertainment, *it is increasingly valued as a delicacy in other parts of the world.*

FRIEND OF THE FAMILY

Neither boy can remember a time when he has not known the other; their houses are separated only by two long sections of chainlink fence and a high-strung Schnauzer bitch named Tiffany who patrols the Perlmutters' backyard, directing her piercing bark toward any person or animal who comes within fifty yards of her territory. The two families have been close since their mothers discovered that they were both due in September of 1986, one with the boy who would be Gabriel and the other with the girl she would name Lacey. Marnie and Elizabeth still swim and talk; Frank and Jack swap power tools; Lacey plays surrogate mother to Jackie. It is strange, then, that the boys, only fourteen months apart, have never really been friendly. Gabriel, when given the choice, has always gravitated toward the older kids in the neighborhood, who spurn roly-poly little Tommy Harrison. Gabe himself has never really trusted Tommy, with his incessant blinking and puppydog obsequiousness and outrageous brags. And, since the time Gabe told the other kids about the younger boy's demonstrably false claim to have a bowling alley in his basement – that is, since the nickname "Lying Tommy" made its way back to the bearer – he's been uncomfortably sure the feeling must be mutual.

17   Friend *or* Friends *was once common in almost every North American Family.*
Competition from Entertainment *appears to have thinned its numbers substantially.*

SEE ALSO:
(018) ANGST   (060) HIERARCHY   (084) MEANING, SEARCH FOR
(094) NATURE VS. NURTURE   (104) PROVIDENCE   (110) RECOGNITION
(136) WHATEVER

GRAVITY

The garage is where it first happened. He was supposed to clean it out for like ten dollars or something. My mom had sent me over to borrow an edge-trimmer, and Mrs. Hungate told me to go into the garage and ask him to help me find it. At first I couldn't see him. It was dim in there with the single bulb and all. Even though it was the kind of garage with windows, it was a grey day outside at the end of August. I remember there was a tennis ball strung from the ceiling like a hangman. Kind of creepy. Then I heard this clackety-clack sound from the other side of the car. I walked around the rear bumper and saw him squatting there on the concrete pad, arranging aerosol cans in a milk-crate. He jumped a little at the sound of his name. He was like Do you want something? and I told him about the edge-trimmer. He softened after that; I guess I had just scared him. We were sixteen and hadn't talked in probably a decade, since the time I pushed him into the pool for trying to give me a wedgie. Or at least in the year since my dad had died. Gabe was a foot taller than he had been back when I'd had my crush on him, and something else…more secretive, I guess. Quieter. He got the edge-trimmer out from wherever it was and put it in my hand and said, "Anything else?" I think it was raining outside. I told him I was sorry about his parents. He stared at me like he might slap me. "I'd rather not talk about it," he said. I told him I had been there. Boy, had I. But when I apologized, he said, "Don't be sorry." Next thing I'm sitting on the hood of his mom's Volvo with his waist in between my knees and we're kissing. I had kissed boys before, but not like that. Not like fighting and kissing at the same time, with our belt buckles scraping together. When I said I'd better go, what I meant was *Tell me to stay*, but he didn't. I spent a couple weeks waiting in agony before he called me on the phone and said "So what are you doing?"

18 *The attraction between two bodies can be calculated by multiplying the quotient of the product of their combined mass and the square of the distance between them by the universal gravitational constant, G.*

GRIEF

Less than a month after Gabe's accident she was back in the gym in her pep squad whites, her feet falling into the complicated floor-work as though she'd only been gone a weekend. If she'd lost anything, it was only the inside track for next year's head cheerleading position, the goodwill that would have accrued from four additional weeks of closeness with the other girls. She would never have imagined, or desired, that the sympathy they now felt toward her had virtually guaranteed her the spot. That her best friend and closest competitor Michelle DuPlessis was ready to step aside for her. Lacey didn't let the subject come up, didn't give Michelle an opening. Instead, she hurled herself brightly into the new routines, clapping, slapping her hips, shaking her ass, springing into the air, dropping to the parquet, spiraling back up, her index finger thrust into the air, her exultant smile so well-rehearsed as to seem completely spontaneous. She sweated a little more than usual – she was out of shape and this was strenuous work – but she resisted the urge to put her hands on her thighs during downtime. At the end of practice, when it was time to make the pyramid, the girls insisted that she reclaim her place at the top. She was, after all, the lightest. As she rose, lofted by the soft hands on her legs and back, she forgot, for a moment, that she'd ever been gone at all. From the top of the pyramid, it was hard to imagine that anyone died ever. And if later she slumped a little bit on the locker-room bench, waiting for the other girls to finish showering before she took off her clothes, no one was so gauche as to let her know they noticed.

19 *Slow to adapt to the ecological upheavals of the American century, Grief now thrives only in isolation. The study of Grief is further complicated by its nocturnal Habits, and by the fact that no Grief is like any other.*

SEE ALSO:
(024) COMMITMENT   (030) DEPRESSION   (034) DIVORCE
(042) FISCAL RESPONSIBILITY   (044) FREEDOM
(084) MEANING, SEARCH FOR   (086) MIDLIFE CRISIS
(114) RESIGNATION

GUILT

"Oh, you know....Since pretty much as far back as I can remember." And how far back can you remember? "Everything's a question with you guys, isn't it?" Does that make you uncomfortable? "No, no. It's just..." He laughs, not wholly convincingly. "Okay, you want a story, I'll give you a story. We were all on a school trip to the roller-skating rink. Galaxy of Sports, it was called. Gabe and Lacey were in Second Grade or something, I must have been in first, maybe even kindergarten. There was this girl I was crazy about, with the hair-bow and the curls that were begging to be pulled. Jenny. Jenny Lehotsky Why are you looking at me like that?" I'm not looking at you like anything, Thomas. Keep going. "Well, I thought maybe Jenny and I could go roller-skating, maybe hold hands. I mean Gabe and my sister were probably already doing Olympic routines at the center of the rink, but this girl was scared or something. She spent, I don't know...an hour hanging around the snack bar. And then she took some money out of her pocket and proceeded to clean them out. They sold these candy-sticks, these barber-shop spirals, lemon swirled with lime, butterscotch swirled with cream, and when she turned around with a huge handful I swear it was the most beautiful thing I'd ever seen. She starts handing the candy sticks out to her friends, friends who unwrap them and eat them incredibly slowly, making those noises of enjoyment. Yum. Slurp. Mmm. My dad, of course, has taken the position that he's already shelling out five bucks for the damn skate rental, and no I may not have any money for snacks. So naturally I ask my beloved, you know, you've got like fifty of those, could I have one? You may not, she says. And I watch her put the rest of them in the locker where her shoes are. Well, what am I supposed to do, when she goes off to skate with her friends and leaves the locker unlocked? Your honor, I plead guilty. I stole a butterscotch candy-stick and hid behind the whack-a-mole game to eat it. But here's the interesting part: I couldn't. I took one bite, and immediately I saw my dad's face, my dad kneeling at the communion rail, that why-me-lord look he got, and the candy just turned to ash in my mouth. I went and turned myself into the teacher and asked to be punished. She probably thought it was hilarious, this little kid looking for absolution for stealing like two cents' worth of candy that probably should have been given to him anyway. But she bit her tongue and told me to go tell my victim what I'd done. Which is the last time I ever stole anything. Not to mention the last time Michelle ever talked to me." Jenny? "Right. Jenny."

20 *Family-watchers generally agree that Guilt is essential for a healthy ecosystem, but recent genomic variation has led to some ruptures in the parent-offspring relationship.*

HABITS, BAD

You'll see them first thing in the morning, like dew on the lawns, and last thing at night, in the gaps where the motion-sensors won't detect them. They believe they're invisible like this, in the shadows, but if you study the postures of the figures hunched on front stoops and in bathroom windows by box-fans and slumped in lawnchairs out back, you will recognize congressmen, judges, PTA chairs, pillars of the community, sometimes even your own parents or children – the secret smokers. Each cigarette is a stitch binding their lives more tightly together: the cigarettes Jack sneaks behind the modest bungalow literally on the other side of the tracks from the old place on the water; the cigarettes that drove Frank's blood pressure up by imperceptible degrees; the cigarettes Gabe chain-smokes on his long nocturnal drives to wherever it is he disappears to; the ones Lacey smells on his breath that make her want to ask him to choose, her or Philip Morris, even as she leans in for another kiss.

Depending on parent genotype, the crossbreeding of a Bad Habit *and* Boredom *will result in either* Chemistry *or* Entertainment.

SEE ALSO:
(056) HABITS, GOOD

HABITS, GOOD

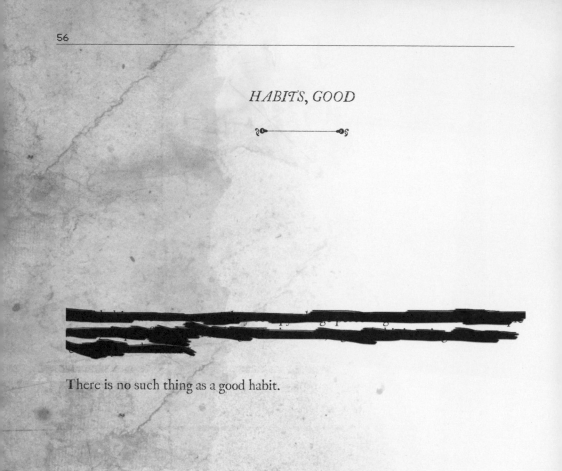

There is no such thing as a good habit.

For identification of all habits, see Habits, Bad.

HEIRLOOM

It wasn't like I planned it, exactly. Sometimes in the summer it was just, you know, ride out to Suffolk County at night, see what comes your way. Out there, the parking lots went on for acres. You could just smoke a tree and watch the sky, the planes streaking in to Islip, if you were feeling that certain way. Or you might ride out there with some of your boys and just fuck with people. I never really got in anybody's face like that before, but, I don't know, a gun's got a mind of its own. Like in *Lord of the Rings*; like it's using you to complete its destiny. Or I don't know, maybe I was just fucked up. The gun was my uncle's, before he went upstate. I borrowed it off my cousin after I got jumped by some Spanish dudes outside the takeout one day. For protection and whatnot. I didn't really plan to use it, just to keep it in my waistband to show, if necessary. And then I'm sitting out there all red-eyed on the trunk of my boy's car in a parking lot in Suffolk County, and he nudges me like, see that? And I look across all those empty puddles of light at this tall, ghost-looking shadow coming toward us. And my boy's like, "You see that? He just showed you the finger, son." I knew it wasn't true, but the kid was walking like he owned the island and didn't have to think about nothing. I said, "I'll give him something to think about." I walked up alongside him and asked for a dollar, like for a Coke. He just kept on walking, paint all on his pants like some artschool fag. I'm like, you hear me? And he just says, "I heard you." But like looking somewhere to the left of my head, all spacey. So I'm like, hear this, motherfucker. It felt good in my hand, the waffled grip, like all the years of Duck Hunt and then Bond had been preparing me. He was probably my age. It was like some movie I can't remember the name of: the two of us, same height, same build, different shades, moving through our different lives to this one moment where we measured each other's strength. And he won. Because of the look in his eyes, that look in them like, just go on ahead and shoot me. That made it real. I said, "Fuck this" and ran to the car and we peeled out. Later, I tried to lie, say I got his wallet, but my boy asked to see it. All I had to show was eight bucks and a bus transfer, which I'd had when we rode out there.

23 *The reappearance of the* Heirloom, *which happens only once per generation, is not to be missed by connoisseurs of* Meaning.

SEE ALSO:
(018) ANGST   (020) BOREDOM   (022) CHEMISTRY
(060) HIERARCHY   (092) MYTHOLOGY   (094) NATURE VS. NURTURE
(108) REBELLION   (130) TRADITION   (136) WHATEVER

HIERARCHY

There were two kinds of people, Tommy reflected as he walked past the big, detached, Cape-Cod-style houses, the porches with their extravagant pumpkins: those who are It and those who are Not-It. Differentiation began at an early age, in backyards and playgrounds. Some Not-Its, through an elaborate and invisible sensory apparatus, were able to intuit the precise instant a game began, and to shout "Not It" to the world. The rest learned fairly quickly to chime in whenever the call of "Not It" arose, and thereby to escape solitude. Not-Its called the games. Not-Its set the rules. Not-Its grew up to own houses of the type Tommy was now passing, spacious and freestanding and painted to look as though they'd always been there, with pumpkins large enough to feed entire third-world villages. It was mid-October, and the streets near school were empty; having skipped sixth period, he was too early for the flood of Not-It kids that would sluice down these sidewalks at three p.m. When the wind stirred, the leaves made a pleasant scudding sound on the concrete. He veered off the sidewalk to kick at a leaf-pile. Tommy was surrounded by Not-Its. His dad, for example. And Gabe. The first to shout, the ones with the best toys. His sister and Mrs. Hungate fell in effortlessly with the Not-It camp. But Tommy, through some quirk of genetics, had always been an It. Every group needed one. The one whose voice lingered alone and false in the air when all the others had faded: "Not It!" The one who stayed behind when the Not-Its ran away. He swerved again to kick at another pile of leaves, doubtless raked by the laborers imported from Plainview and Hicksville and Queens to keep the yards tidy. He was hoping to uncover a mulchy underworld of worms and wriggling, but of course it hadn't rained for weeks.

24

Believed by ancient cultures to ward off the evil spirits of Anarchy *and* Misfortune
(cf. CLAN, COURT AND CLOISTER: A POCKET ALMANAC*),* Hierarchy *is
now seen as vulnerable to attack from many of the great predators that stalk the North
American Family.*

HOLIDAY

Nowadays we split them all, right down the middle of the day, so that the kids might, for example, be with Jack until noon on Christmas, and then with me for the turkey dinner and the evening afterward. Soon Gabe will be off at college, and then Jackie, and it hardly seems worth getting a big tree anymore. That was always Jack's thing anyway. We're paying for the high ceilings, was his reasoning, why not use them? Every year he and Gabe would come back from their expedition with a tree bigger than the last. It would take the three of us just to get it through the door. Still, I have to admit, with all the lights and all of the million Christmas ornaments Jack's mother had given to us from her private hoard, it looked beautiful. Some nights when the kids had ostensibly gone to sleep he and I would lie back on the sofa and just watch it. I remember the way the big back window doubled the lights, like a multicolored galaxy in a slick black sky. Our first Christmas Eve after we moved out of the city, back when the tree was modest, we were lying like that taking a breather before putting the presents out. Gazing at the tree, at the glitter-strewn star we'd just placed on top, I still felt fat from the pregnancy, but it didn't seem to matter to Jack. His hands had begun to explore the skin between my navel and my pantyline when Gabe appeared on the stairs crying. He must have been about seven. Jackie had just started sleeping through the night. I asked him what was wrong, expecting him to say that he missed the old apartment, that he wanted to move back. Instead he managed to explain, in fits and starts, that he'd been thinking about all the toys we'd given him that he'd abandoned after playing with for a week or two. He'd been thinking about how lonely they must be, sitting at the top of the closet, and how disappointed we must be, and how there were children in Africa who didn't have any toys. I told him it was okay, we would donate the old toys to some kids right here on Long Island who might like them. I barely managed to keep a straight face as I told him to go back to bed, Santa Claus would be here soon. And then as soon as he was gone I found myself crying, too. He was a funny kid like that.

25   Holiday *may be observed as many as eight times a year. A peaceable creature, it abhors confrontation; all conflicts within the pack are settled via high-frequency communications inaudible to the human ear.*

HOME

They came to Long Island in search of sunlight. Not the kind that trickled down like water through the fingers of a skyline, but the kind that spread like butter across a green expanse of lawn. They came to Long Island for the relative quiet, the soothing bugsong in summer, in winter the cold crash of waves. They came for the view of those waves, for the big picture window in the living room that looked out over the pool, the trees, the backyard, the breakwater. They came for the community, the neighborhood, the schools. All it cost was a thirty-year mortgage, club dues and greens fees, and train-fare to the city five days a week. There were good years in these houses and in these yards. There were pickup basketball games in the driveways, with the kids. There were parties. There were Halloweens and Thanksgivings. And if, after the switch to standard time, they got home well after dark; and if gradually the kids became strangers; and if when the lights were out they only fell asleep exhausted…well, was that so different from what their own parents had done, chasing their own dreams of America?

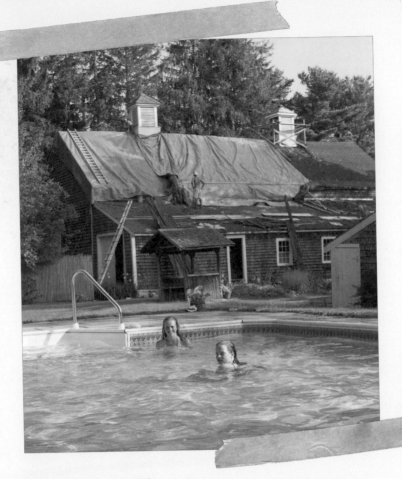

2b   *Once highly localized in its* Habits, *the* Home *has become increasingly nomadic in the last century. It has been known to travel great distances to secure a source of* Mortgages, *on which it subsists.*

INFIDELITY

Tommy made things up for the grief counselor, told him what he thought he wanted to hear. I wanted to be just like him, he said. It's my fault, he said. Why? Because if I could have been there in time, I could have dialed 911 and Dad would still be alive. He thought he was being clever. Because what he would never, never, never tell the therapist or anyone else was that there had been times lately when he had secretly wished for something like this to happen. His dad, after all, had been cheating on his mom for half a year – he had overheard him whispering into the phone, when he thought no one was listening. To Tommy it felt as though, in some obscure way, his dad had been cheating on him. The code of honor had been breached, and would never quite make sense again.

27

Infidelity *is the hollow-boned relative of the lesser-known* Fidelity.

INNOCENCE

Jackie continues to make solid academic progress this term. Her unusual verbal gifts and acute imagination have translated into some remarkable creative writing, although her spelling remains unorthodox, perhaps willfully so. Certainly Jackie is a voracious reader, when allowed to choose her own books from the school library. In our Social Studies unit we are encouraging all of our students to try to see historical events from multiple perspectives. While Math is sometimes a challenge for Jackie, consolidating basic skills will help her tackle more complex problems. Any parental support with homework would, of course, be welcome. But our major goals for the remainder of the year are social in nature. Although Jackie is often gregarious with adults, she tends to alternate between somewhat withdrawn and rather dominant behavior patterns within her peer group. This is typical of an earlier developmental stage than the highly socialized phase many of her classmates have entered. As we discussed at her midyear conference, her difficulty forming and sustaining close relationships with other girls may be related to unresolved feelings about her parents' divorce. Her controlled demeanor appears to mask a child of extreme sensitivity. Although we understand Jackie's resistance, and wish to respect her unique spirituality, we continue to recommend that she meet with the school counselor regularly and that she attend our monthly grief lunches. It is the school's belief that learning to adapt to change at a young age will promote health of mind and body throughout the many challenges our students will encounter in their lifetimes.

28   *Although the life-span of Innocence was once believed to be only a few years in duration, recent findings reveal that Innocence can persist in a state of semi-hibernation decades after its initial burst of activity has ended.*

INTEGRITY

What attracts people to one another? The question has puzzled humans throughout the ages. Still we know little, except that the nature of attraction is irrational. Hypothetically speaking, a successful careerwoman in her early forties should have little rational incentive to stray from a marriage that has yielded two healthy children. Even were the most virile man to express interest, she would hardly be able to find time for a dalliance amid her busy schedule. Indeed, time is probably the one thing missing from her marriage (again, hypothetically). Yet it has been documented that such a woman will find herself attracted to someone other than her spouse—even to someone subjectively characterized as undistinguished in appearance and self-absorbed in personality. Perhaps it is this self-absorption that proves irresistible to our hypothetical woman as she approaches hypothetical middle age; perhaps, contrary to all of our earlier hypotheses, such a woman is looking for someone who does not desire or need her in anything other than a physical way. Perhaps this quality attracts her precisely because, on some level, she wishes she shared it. But here we come close to reducing attraction, infinite in its variety, to a single formula. In understanding what animates erotic desire, we are no closer than were our ancestors, who looked for their answers to the stars.

29

Members of this dying breed may bear little resemblance to one another. In the wild, however, Integrity recognizes its own by the strong jaws and steely eyes endemic to the species.

INTIMACY

This would be right after the first time they went all the way. Which, just so you know, was Lacey's first time ever. It was a few months after her dad had died all unannounced like that; her mom had like gone to the city for the day or something. "You're in charge, Lacey," Mrs. Hungate had said – as if that cretinous little brother of hers would ever let her tell him what to do. Plus when Gabe was around it wasn't like Lacey had a whole lot of attention left over for anyone else, you know? Picture Lying Tommy telling her he's going to the library or to volunteer at the orphanage or whatever and then slipping off to do whatever it was he was really doing. Lacey is alone, except for Gabe there with her in that totally amazing house her dad paid for. He's just been inside her. She hasn't loved it, but she loves him, and now they're lying naked together with the fall light, that totally clear morning sunlight that comes off the Sound filling up the lace curtains she's pulled so no one can see in, and all of a sudden, boom, he's totally there. He's propped up beside her and he's fixed her in his eyes like he never does with anyone else. It's what she lives for, she'll tell me, that look like he can see right down into you. (As if I would ever have any idea what she was talking about. As if he would ever turn that look on me.) Anyway, he moves. She thinks he's reaching for another condom from the nightstand, but really he's grabbing that Sharpie he always carried, and before she can say anything he's drawing a bird freehand on her upper arm, a hawk I think. And in its claws a heart. Not a valentine heart but like with veins and everything. I know, I know, she showed it to me afterward and I was like, can you get any cheesier. But secretly I was jealous. That became their thing, I guess, because sometimes after practice, when the lockerroom had emptied out, I would catch a glimpse of her all alone in the shower stall, with these wild designs all done in marker on the hidden spaces of her abdomen, the ones that don't show when your clothes are on. And whatever those bitches told her later, he never brought out the Sharpie for me, which is how I knew we'd made a mistake.

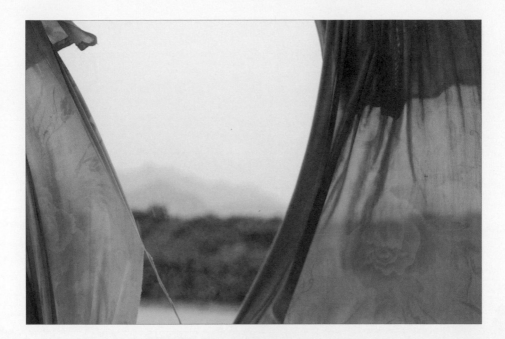

30   *By day, this quiet creature lies motionless near watering holes, where the noise and movement of larger beasts distract potential predators. Only when night falls does* Intimacy *awaken and begin its search for sustenance.*

IRONY

The new linoleum was the last of the improvements they made to the house that year, and after her son found her husband sprawled on it in the cardiac arrest that would end his life, Marnie wanted to rip it up with her bare hands. She wanted to never walk on it again. She blamed that linoleum, somehow. And she blamed herself, because when she'd called from the city that night to say she'd be getting home late from the alumni dinner, and heard the answering machine pick up, she assumed he was out, rather than dying in the kitchen. He still went out often, for a man his age. She had no reason to feel guilty, there was nothing she could have done, was Elizabeth's take on things. During the first month of widowhood, Marnie walked over to the Hungates' nearly every night. But the conversations were like television. Afterwards, she felt even more lonely. Marnie blamed her own inability to be really honest about her feelings about Frank; not for a minute did she think that maybe it had something to do with Elizabeth.

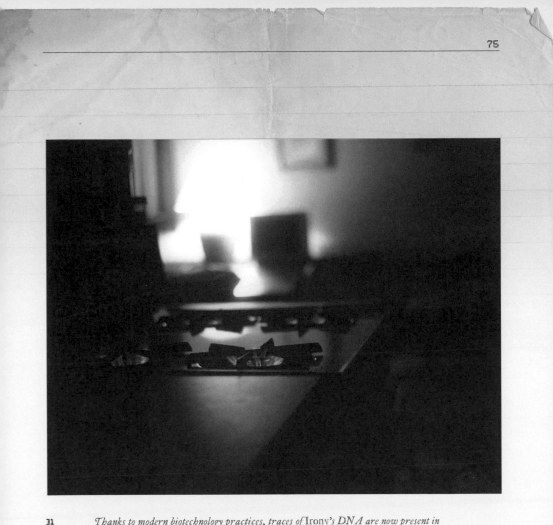

31   *Thanks to modern biotechnology practices, traces of* Irony's DNA *are now present in the genome of almost all the other organisms that comprise the North American Family.*

LOVE

You'd seen him when they wheeled him in, you would've said forty-eight hours to maybe seventy-two at the outside. Even under the sheet on the gurney, you could tell from the way the fluids had begun to seep, like the way grease from a cheesesteak will turn the bag almost clear where it soaks through. Anytime you're talking about second- or third-degree, you're talking about a lot of fluid loss. That's the major danger. Think of a piece of meat that's been overcooked. That's all we are, really. Now you have Dr. Ross running around like the Queen of Spain because her case-study's coming out in *JAMA*. And I'll give her credit for pioneering the technique – there's some who won't, but what do I know about it? But there's a big difference between keeping someone from dying and giving them a reason to live. And since that seems to be the point of your question, let me just mention his family and that little cheerleader who made the cookies. They were there every day when I come on, and she was there when I went off.

32   *Though hardly the most visible member of its kingdom,* Love *has never been as endangered as alarmists would have us believe. Without it, new research confirms, the entire Family would cease to function.*

MATERIAL

One house, three cars, four sets of clothes, gratuitous amounts of shoes, daily medications, weekly groceries, glossy monthlies, a year's supply of firewood for the wood-burning stove, a garage worth of tennis rackets and basketballs, a lifetime of cigarettes. Honey can I, Daddy can't I, Dad why can't I, won't you, will you? Please would you write a check, please can I have some cash, please could we put your name down for a small donation? Of course Frank would. He can. He could. For cellphones and Palm Pilots and personal computers, he'd shell out. For cornerstones and uniforms and meals on wheels for the elderly. These things cost money, but then that's why he worked. In the end, it's always easier to say yes.

33   *Although* Material's *impact on other species continues to puzzle observers, it has proven difficult for any ecosystem to flourish in its complete absence.*

SEE ALSO:
(016) ADULTHOOD   (036) ENTERTAINMENT
(042) FISCAL RESPONSIBILITY   (052) GUILT   (064) HOME
(090) MORTGAGE   (136) WHATEVER

MATERNAL INSTINCT

There's a plywood wall, six feet high by ten wide, in the backyard of the house occupied by Elizabeth and Jackie and, until recently (on Mondays, Tuesdays, Thursdays, and every other weekend, anyway), Gabe. Elizabeth had it built and, whatever happens to him, will never have it removed, because it is not hers to remove. Moisture off the Sound and extreme temperatures have faded the paint and warped the wood until it curls at the edges like paper. The figures, though, are still visible: faces, flags, birds, bodies, whorls and jags and the name he chose to represent him, Casper, written over and over. Repetition is how he'd learned. She'd heard the bass booming from behind the closed door of his room. She'd seen the way he'd abandoned the GameCube, the way he stooped over his sketchpad. And she'd figured, at least he wasn't on drugs, as Marnie Harrison claimed half of the kids at the high school were. She'd figured, better under her own figurative roof than out somewhere doing God knows what, like Marnie's son. Gabe didn't have to thank her. The light in his face as he practiced his…what did he call them?…his throw-ups, his burners, was enough.

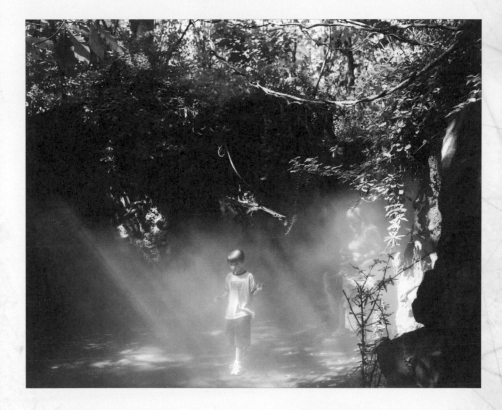

34   Maternal Instinct *hovers near the top of the food chain. Dominant females, who do the hunting for the herd, have been known to attack creatures as formidable as* Depression *and as insignificant as the smallest* Boredom *in order to provide for their young.*

MATURITY

You know, Alphonse, things could be worse. Mom and Dad are talking again and the little tree we got him from the drug store by the hospital makes the window-sill look less lonely, even though the warm weather doesn't seem like Christmas and I bet he's sad he's missing all the sunshine. Yesterday, Alphonse, he said his first thing since it happened, and do you know what? It was to me. Not to Mom or Dad or Lacey. He reached out and grabbed my arm right here above the elbow and he said without moving his lips, "Don't grow up." I bet he would have been smiling if it didn't hurt to smile. Now you might be wondering what he meant by "Don't grow up," but I knew just what he was saying. He was saying, "Don't end up like me," and do you know what, Alphonse? I don't think I will!

35

More retiring than Adulthood, *with which it is so often confused,* Maturity is *associated with* Discipline, Grief, Resignation, *and* Sacrifice.

SEE ALSO:
(020) BOREDOM (024) COMMITMENT (068) INNOCENCE
(076) LOVE (078) MATERIAL (082) PRIVACY
(112) RECONCILIATION (130) TRADITION

MEANING, SEARCH FOR

⟡————⟡

Tall tales Tommy told: that he held brown belts in tae kwon do and jujitsu. That his dad had let him drive the Porsche when he was only 13. That his IQ had been tested at 160. That Gabe Hungate was his best friend. That he and Gabe Hungate were half-brothers, blood brothers. That Gabe Hungate had stolen his Roger Clemens rookie card. That he could make a fire by rubbing two sticks together. That he had once moved a spoon a couple of inches across a table just by thinking about it. That he had lost his virginity in junior high, at sleepaway camp. That he and his dad went golfing every Saturday. That he had been born in Brooklyn. That he could play electric guitar and was getting one from his dad for his birthday. That his dad made over a million dollars per year. That his dad gave one quarter of his income to charity. That his dad secretly worked for the CIA. That his mother was the former Miss Sheepshead Bay. That his sister was adopted. That he was trying out for linebacker. That he would inherit ten million dollars when he turned 18. That he wasn't high right now. That he had already been accepted at Harvard on account of his precocious SAT scores. That any of this would have mattered, if that was actually his dad buried out there in the cemetery, instead of the dummy his dad had used to fake his own death before slipping away to Brazil on a top-secret mission the gravity of which only Tommy, his sole confidante, understood.

36

Search for Meaning *is one of the most commonly occurring organisms in the North American Family. Identifying it is complicated by its chameleon-like ability to mimic other species, such as* Infidelity *or* Material.

MIDLIFE CRISIS

One of those backyard barbecues toward the end of summer. A season of short-ening days, when the specter of school hangs nearby, daring the kids to name it, to make it real. A season when Japanese lanterns have again become de rigeur. When if, like Elizabeth Hungate in one of her sudden and misguided fevers of trying to change her life, you've had your son drag the moldy box of Japanese lanterns from the garage out to the curb, you might curse yourself: you should have known you'd only have to buy them again. After all, everything comes back eventually. Haven't you witnessed this scene before: the sway of the little colored lanterns in the pool's unquiet surface? The drone of the air-conditioner at the side of the house? The yapping dog next door? The cluster of patio chairs the adults have drawn together and abandoned like toys on the lawn while Jack flips the burgers and Marnie goes to make sure Tommy and Gabe are getting along and Frank goes inside to mix more drinks? Elizabeth has been here before. Returning from the bathroom, she's paused at the sliding back door, close enough to feel the cool radiating off it. The lightning bugs are out. Gabe floats nonchalantly in the pool, fully clothed, his shorts bloated with an air-bubble. He's gesturing rudely to Lacey, who's just pushed him in. Lacey she doesn't know about, but Elizabeth can see that beneath her son's merciless teasing, he is already half-in-love with the girl, and it hurts her with a sharpness that almost stops her breathing. Here's another hurt: though she doesn't want to, she can feel Frank standing behind her. She wishes she could melt into the glass, become transparent too, a thing people only notice in passing. She wants to tell Gabe never to fall in love. But she won't. Besides: he always has to learn everything the hard way.

37

An erratic Maturity *pattern characterizes the* Midlife Crisis*: it may remain a manageable size for years, only to reach its full stature in a few turbulent days.*

SEE ALSO:

(016) ADULTHOOD   (032) DISCRETION   (034) DIVORCE
(038) FAMILY VALUES   (048) GRAVITY   (070) INTEGRITY
(080) MATERNAL INSTINCT   (094) NATURE VS. NURTURE
(098) PARTINGS   (134) VULNERABILITY

MOMENT OF CLARITY

What the fuck have we been doing with ourselves?

SEE ALSO:
(068) INNOCENCE   (114) RESIGNATION

MORTGAGE

Jack hasn't been working since the separation. "On hiatus," they call it at the firm. He cancelled all of his appointments an hour before he and Elizabeth sat the kids down to tell them, and then it was the weekend. On Monday he woke up in a hotel room and, for the first time since he passed the New York bar, called in sick. On Tuesday, after a morning spent reading and rereading briefs, trying to make the words mean something, he called a meeting with the senior partners to announce his decision. Of course, they pointed out, with his assets halved and his alimony considerable, it was either soldier on at work or get used to being poor. He's stuck with poverty so far – that's why his new house is only nine hundred square feet. Now he spends his days there, watching TV, cleaning compulsively, gardening and making furniture.

39   *Many prospective owners choose to adopt a* Mortgage *in the hope that domesticating this difficult beast in the present might make it easier to housebreak* Security *in the future.*

SEE ALSO:
(028) CUSTODY BATTLE   (032) DISCRETION   (044) FREEDOM
(064) HOME   (078) MATERIAL   (112) RECONCILIATION
(118) SACRIFICE   (130) TRADITION

MYTHOLOGY

The class spent much of December constructing the N.A. Village. The teacher painted a tarpaulin green to represent Land, leaving a blue margin of Water. There was perfectly good land and water beyond the window of the classroom, Jackie wanted to say, but she was called back to help construct Trees from rolled cardboard and tissue paper, and by the time they moved on to Crops, she'd forgotten. Pumpkins made of modeling clay, cornstalks fashioned from pipe cleaners, tiny clay gourds on pipe cleaner vines with tissue paper leaves...Crops took forever. Jackie put hers near the Water, for ease of irrigation. Longhouses were easy enough; everyone brought in a shoebox. They spent a day cutting construction paper bark to cover the logos and shoe sizes. The completed Houses were arranged in a circle, not like the Wagons they'd made in the Pioneers unit, but facing in, toward the center of the Village, where the tribal council would meet. People and Animals came last. People: clothespins colored brown, yarn hot-glued on for hair, felt tunics and tools made of toothpicks. Animals: more modeling clay. People went in the Village and Animals went in the Forest. For protection, Jackie erected a popsicle stick Stockade. When she leaned down so that her head was almost level with the carpet, what she saw was another world. She imagined the People and Animals moving around at night, preparing for an ambush, ravaging the classroom in the dark. Then, a few days before Christmas Break, the class gathered in a semicircle around the Village. "Don't touch," the teacher said. "This is a solemn occasion." She passed out notecards marked Trees, People, and Animals. Jackie, what did I just say? she said. "A very solemn occasion. You see, this is the world in which the N.A.s lived. Before the Europeans came and razed the Trees. Tree people, come forward," she said. Kids with Trees notecards were told to remove the Trees from the tarpaulin. "Without the Trees, where did the Animals go?" Jackie asked. The teacher nodded. "Very astute. Animals people, remove the Animals. Without Animals, the People had no source of food. No, they couldn't eat the Europeans, don't be silly. People people...." Jackie stood up. Outside, it was winter. The playground was a big, white blank. Already, she could see how it all would stretch away. Uninhabited, the Longhouses would crumble. Sans Houses, Crops, People, Animals, and Trees, only a flat expanse of canvas would remain. And by the end of school, kids would be back in the cubby area staging miniature wrestling matches between the clothespin N.A.'s they'd made. They would be reminded to take home their People and Animals, but they would forget, and then they'd get left here: broken Indians, some deer, and a tree on the muddy floor of the cubby area, everything they'd worked so hard on waiting to be thrown away. She pretended not to feel the other kids staring at her, as she began to pluck the People and Animals up off the tarpaulin. She pretended not to hear the teacher say, "Jackie? What on earth are you doing?"

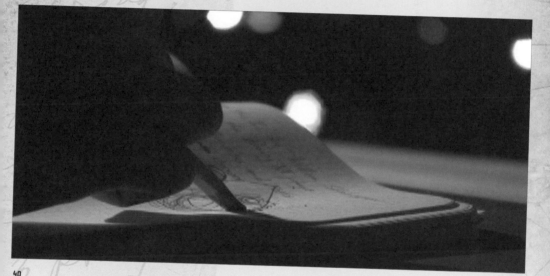

40

Without Mythology, *what would protect the Family from the harshness of the* elements? Tradition? Optimism? Entertainment? *Experiments designed to answer this question have thus far proved disastrous.*

SEE ALSO:
(068) INNOCENCE   (138) YOUTH

NATURE VS. NURTURE

It's tough to say in retrospect whether it was the divorce that made him reckless. He can remember tightrope-walking the third-story beams of a house under construction in the neighborhood years ago. He can remember Lacey yelling at him to come down, and Lying Tommy standing yards behind her, just watching, as though waiting for him to fall. Maybe it was genetic, although if anyone was a by-the-book player it was his dad. But maybe he got it from his mom. Maybe the divorce had just drawn out his latent tendencies in that direction, sent him spinning out past the point of acceptable risk. But then there was Lacey. So maybe it was when he got mugged that time at the LIRR station. There's something liberating about realizing that you can stare into the black hole of a handgun and still feel nothing. Because it was only afterwards that he began to court disaster in earnest. That he began to turn off the headlights in the middle of the highway. That he graduated from bombing municipal walls around Stony Brook to sneaking into city trainyards in the dead of night. It was easy, with his mom and dad not talking. You just told each parent you were with the other. It was almost like freedom, except that nothing gave him pleasure anymore, except the trains. So maybe it was that, the incident with the gun. Whatever the case, he doesn't feel fearless anymore. Because it's not death you ultimately have to worry about. It's pain.

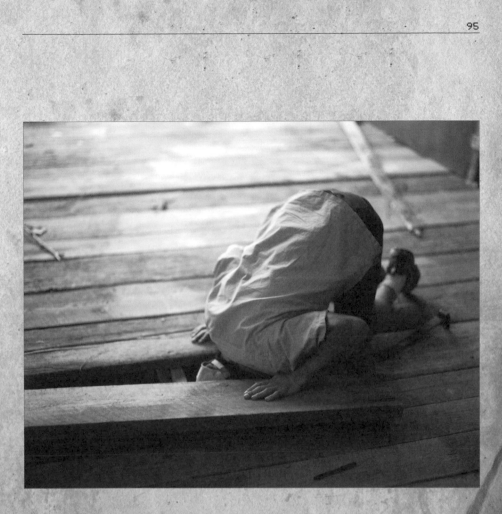

41   *The exact character of this unlikely hybrid has puzzled Family-watchers for years.*

OPTIMISM

Marnie pads barefoot into a cold kitchen and lights the burner underneath some water. Her first few attempts have been disasters: whites dissolving, little wisps of yolk reaching out for the walls of the pot. Frank's away on a golfing junket, and last night, on the phone, she almost gave in and told him. His teaspoon of vinegar hasn't helped. This is the way we talk when he's on the road, she thinks. I confess my failings, and he gets to tell me everything I'm missing, everything I'm doing wrong. She cracks the egg into a small bowl, careful not to break the yolk. Even two years later, he won't talk about the miscarriage. The burner's blue crown hums in the predawn dim. She reaches for a wooden spoon. Bubbles rise like loosed balloons toward the surface as she stirs. A pang in her abdomen. When Frank used that word, centripetal, it had made her think at first of her father's desk chair, the leather one that revolved on casters. As a little girl, on trips to his office downtown, she had climbed into it with her dolls. She had spun around and around, her shoe scuffing the wall. The G-force made her feel like an astronaut. But hadn't it pulled them outward, until she felt she would, at any second, fly off? "Trust me," Frank had said. He calmly explained that that had been an illusion. It was just centripetal force, he said, combining with the first law of motion to create the feeling you were being pulled away from the center. Now Marnie tips the egg into the centrifuge of water. She takes a breath. She reaches beneath her nightgown and places a hand on the taut space beneath her navel, where their first child, finally, is growing. "Trust me," he said. Centripetal literally means center-seeking. She is slightly disappointed to discover that he's right. The center does hold. In the midst of all that boiling water, the egg's innards spin like a tiny, soft sun. So why does her universe feel smaller today? It would have been their little boy's birthday, had she carried him to term. Blue balloons. You weren't supposed to tell anyone until three months in. She had broken that rule then, but now she knows better. Another month will pass before she'll tell Frank. She wants to be certain. But she already has a name picked out: Lacey. Funny, she thinks (though he undoubtedly would have reminded her that funny wasn't what she meant, exactly). Here I've been telling myself everything was falling apart, when I just didn't realize what I was falling toward was the center.

Optimism *lives so long as to seem, to the human observer, practically immortal – but unlike that of other creatures, the development of* Optimism *proceeds in reverse. That is,* Optimism *is enormous at birth, and gradually shrinks to its microscopic adult size.*

PARTINGS (AMICABLE AND ACRIMONIOUS)

The look on his face, his beautiful face that beneath the bandages was now yellow, green and grey, a raw scar. The high-pitched sound that came from his mouth when she entered his field of vision. The closing of his eyes, the tightening of the corners of his mouth. The nurse had to give him another shot of Demerol so that he would relax his face. This was how any mother would feel. She should never have encouraged the graffiti. Inside, she was collapsing, like a sail rent from top to bottom, but she told herself she couldn't show weakness. Instead she placed her hand on top of his bandaged head, with no more weight than a thought. She said, "Oh, honey." She said, "I love you. I'm here. I love you." She willed him to hear it, to take to heart these words, filled with a depth of feeling she hadn't experienced since his birth. She hadn't noticed Jack come in, and jumped a little when she felt his arm around her shoulder. She didn't open her eyes or cease her murmuring or shake him off. She could feel his chest rising and falling against her upper arm, and she leaned her head against it, lightly, willing to believe, for a moment at least, that this was what it was there for.

Locked in Sibling Rivalry, *the two subspecies of* Parting *are unable to coexist in the same habitat. However, despite the characteristics that distinguish the two, each is capable of mutating into the other over time.*

SEE ALSO:
(034) DIVORCE   (042) FISCAL RESPONSIBILITY   (050) GRIEF
(076) LOVE   (080) MATERNAL INSTINCT   (102) PRIVACY
(122) SECURITY   (130) TRADITION

PHASE

Once upon a time in a faroff kindom there lived
a girl named Jacqueline. Her father was king,
her mother was queen, and her brother, more often
than not, was prince, which made her a princesse.
Princesse Jacqueline loved to talk, to tell jokes,
and to pritend to be a monkey. One thing this princesse
did not love was to be a lone. They were charmed by
her way with a story and her monkey dance, and
endulged her fear of solotude. Who, given the choise,
would chuise to be a lone? But a bewichment began
to fall over the land, so graduelly the princesse
can't tell you exackly when it started. First a
mosterious illnesse overtook her brother, the prince.
He began to keep secrets from her and to send her away
when she nokt on his door. THEN the queen and the
king didint love each other eny more and they split
the cassle in 2. Princesse Jacqueline found herself
under a spell that trapd her in a glasse box, so even
when she could see there were peepul a round her,
they couldnt ~~bre der~~ hear her. The princesse grew
very angry. Sometimes she would bang her hands
agenst the glass. Sometimes she would screme,
because she had read that certin high notes could brake
glass. The childrin of the land grew fearfull of her,
because they thot this was the way she was allways.
Even at her most dispairing, tho, the girl new in her
heart that the spell would be broken someday, and that
she would live happyly ever after, because that was the

the way it happend in evry story.

44   *With their keen senses,* Youth *are more apt to recognize that they have encountered a wild* Phase *than are adults.*

PRIVACY

When the nurse came in at the end of her shift to change the bedpan and replace the IV bags, the girl had vanished like a night-spirit, leaving behind only a chair pulled close to the bed, a welter of crumpled tissues, and an unfinished crossword puzzle. The patient, for his part, was still asleep. His hand on top of the blanket was unburned, a child's hand. She turned it gingerly over to check that the needle was secure and was surprised to find, inked on the palm, a messy blue heart, the Valentine's kind. The next afternoon, during his sponge-bath, she would be careful to avoid this area, as it seemed to mean something to the patient.

45   *Experts disagree about whether this fragile organism is rapidly vanishing from the landscape or merely evolving into a hardier species.*

SEE ALSO:

(024) COMMITMENT   (040) FIDELITY   (048) GRAVITY
(050) GRIEF   (056) HABITS, GOOD   (072) INTIMACY
(076) LOVE   (082) MATURITY   (128) TENDERNESS

PROVIDENCE

That winter, shortly before the string of break-ins in the big shoreside houses came to its abrupt end, The Honorable Robert Perlmutter was awakened from a nap on the leather couch in his study by the creak of the kitchen doors below. Had he been more alert, he might not have shouted, "Hello?" but in his half-waking state some part of him was convinced it must have been one of the neighbor boys returning home from school. Hearing nothing else, he rose. His arthritis ached as he crossed the room to the window. He remembered that his own boys were grown, and gone, and that his only daughter still lay where he'd said good-bye to her 28 years earlier, in a graveyard under the flight paths to LaGuardia. He remembered that one of the neighbor boys was in the intensive care unit. He remembered the crime report in the paper. And he was surprised when he saw the flash of pale neck on the figure sprinting toward his hedge. Justice was blind, and so forth, but he had just assumed that the prowler would be a Negro.

46   *Skeptics have long dismissed* Providence *as a figment of* Mythology, *and yet sightings – always in the wilderness, always uncorroborated – persist.*

QUESTIONS, NAGGING

Who did Elizabeth sleep with?
What does Lacey see in that boy?
Why "Casper"?
Is there life after death?
What is Jackie doing in this story?
Why does anyone smoke cigarettes?

47   *These household pests have plagued the Family throughout its history, and have proven impervious to radiation and all other forms of Security.*

REBELLION

A lark at first, squirreling through the opening where the storm fence didn't quite reach the ground. Telling myself I only wanted to know I could do it, if I wanted to, just like when I was flirting with Michelle Duplessis in the parking lot outside the gym while Lacey was inside cheering. I didn't really mean for anything to happen. But then why had I patrolled the perimeter four times before, looking for a way in? Why had I brought my backpack and the pocketful of good caps? Why did I let her go down on me in the darkness behind the windshield? No one ever tells you there's such a thing as a sad blowjob. And the truth is it's never enough, nothing's ever enough, except bombing my name in wet red letters onto the side of a siderailed car, top-to-bottom burning, when everything evaporates but the hiss and the smell of paint. Everything but myself, all alone out here where the arcs of the nearest security lights don't quite overlap.

48   Rebellion, *common to every habitat, aids the long-term functioning of the Family by clearing out the dead and dying.*

RECOGNITION

Tommy had been a straight-A kid when the boy two doors down was making his way methodically through his parents' neglected liquor cabinet, drinking the bottles down halfway and filling them back up with water. And when, in the summer after his Eighth-Grade year, he tried once more to ingratiate himself with the older boy, the idol of his youth, Gabriel saw right through Tommy's stories about summer camp, about smoking weed, about eating some mushrooms once – not a lot, but enough that he thought he might have started to see visuals. It began to seem to Tommy that he, who worked harder at school and was bigger and stronger and, at least on paper, smarter, deserved some acknowledgement, and so what if he bent the truth sometimes? But poor, troubled Gabe was the older one and got the girls and the attention, which beat trophies and grades as soundly as rock beats scissors. And when their families fell apart, within a season of each other, it was Gabe who got the sympathy, and the bribes from his oblivious mom and dad: the car, for example, and the applause for how well he was taking everything. When Tommy made up a little white lie about how his late father had discovered the Supremes, people recoiled in disgust. When Gabe wanted to vandalize walls, they built him a wall to vandalize. And when he broke into a trainyard and got what he had coming to him, he was tragic, romantic, a victim. And if he had died that night, Tommy knew, the dead kid would still have been the winner in the great attention sweepstakes, even if the living one had nailed himself to a cross. By that time, Tommy had nearly stopped going to class, and whatever time wasn't spent testing the locks of neighborhood backdoors and the credulity of pawnshop owners was spent hotboxing cars in the lot behind the C-Store... as though his real life was nothing more than an attempt to catch up with his fictional one. Pot, at least, would have been something the two boys had in common, except that Gabe had already said goodbye to all that, and moved on to somewhere further out of reach.

49   Recognition *and* Sibling Rivalry *rarely coexist in the same eco-system.*

SEE ALSO:
(018) ANGST   (038) FAMILY VALUES   (046) FRIEND OF THE FAMILY
(052) GUILT   (060) HIERARCHY   (084) MEANING, SEARCH FOR
(116) RUMOR   (120) SECRET   (136) WHATEVER

RECONCILIATION

Jackie's in the waiting area with her lion, rubbing his fur, frowning to herself, when her dad appears at the end of the hall. They haven't spoken in a week and a half. That's not out of the ordinary these days, but it bears mentioning because otherwise Jack might not feel so peculiarly moved by the sight of his daughter stroking a toy he'd picked out for her so many Christmases earlier, might not feel a fist forming in his chest. Immediately the awkwardness of seeing each other again after so long a silence evaporates. He's never felt more like a father than he does now, striding down the corridor toward her, folding her into his body with one crooked arm, kissing the top of her head, calling her "sweetie." "Hi sweetie," he says. She says her mom's in there already.

50 Reconciliation *migrates to landscapes ravaged by* Grief *and* Partings. *By feeding on the carrion these predators leave behind, it encourages the regeneration of a region's flora and fauna.*

RESIGNATION

The sole source of Gabe's charisma was that he'd never much cared what anyone thought, one way or the other. About his car, for example, the little piece-of-shit Geo they would have laughed out of the parking lot at school if they thought it would have bothered him. About his unlikely conversion to sobriety. Or about the threadbare clothes from before the divorce, which he continued to wear even after a growth spurt had put an inch between the cuffs of his pants and the tops of his shoes. But when, having stumbled onto the third rail, he felt the electricity light up his body in a flash of something as close to rapture as to pain, it occurred to him in a strange moment of detachment that, if God granted him life beyond this interminable burning, he would care a great deal about how he looked to other people.

51   *Thriving in climates too damp for its cousin* Rebellion, Resignation *is a mixed blessing for the Family: neither predator nor prey,* Resignation *drains resources without contributing anything to the food chain.*

RUMOR

Supposedly Lying Tommy heard it from Sketchy Dan one afternoon behind the C-Store. For a liar, Tommy tended to take what other people said pretty much at face value. They were chasing down handfuls of Jaz-X Junior ephedrine pills with rum and Mountain Dew and waiting for a buzz to hit. School had just let out, and they were watching kids pass in and out of the smudgy glass doors through the windows of the Sketchmobile. Lying Tommy had just turned old enough to drive but didn't have a car, I heard because his mom didn't trust him behind the wheel. Who would have? Anyway, Tommy said sort of wistfully, hey, there goes my neighbor. And Sketchy Dan said dude, that's the dude I saw getting his knob polished by Michelle DuPlessis outside the basketball game last week. Sounds like a freak coincidence if you ask me, but then, these things usually are.

52

Rumor, *a resilient parasite, feeds on the* Secret *until its host is destroyed. In agricultural areas,* Discretion *is employed as a check on the* Rumor *population.*

SACRIFICE

Jack found it one day among the ailing tomato plants, probably as long as a man's arm...probably someone's pet, escaped or abandoned. It had hollowed out a hole several feet deep beneath the groundcover gone wild at the end of the backyard. Strangely, he didn't find himself repulsed. He kneeled, transfixed by the jade-colored body breathing slowly beneath the green. Later, he investigated on the Internet. *Uromastyx aegyptus*. It got to where, on sunny days when he sat on the back porch drinking domestic beer and pondering the wreck his life had become, the lizard would come near enough to be touched. It would dart away if he moved to hold it, but somehow just touching the ridge along its spine was enough. The lizard's little claws were oddly like human hands. Winter came, and the pallor of the belly began to spread across the jade-green body. Knowing the lizard wouldn't make it through December, he called animal control. A gloved arm reached into the hole and pulled the desperately scrabbling *Uromastyx* out. He found himself thinking of Gabriel's birth, of the delivery room. He found himself holding the lizard, finally, making awkward small talk with the woman from animal control. And he found himself sobbing when the truck pulled away. He wasn't quite sure why. It was only a lizard, after all.

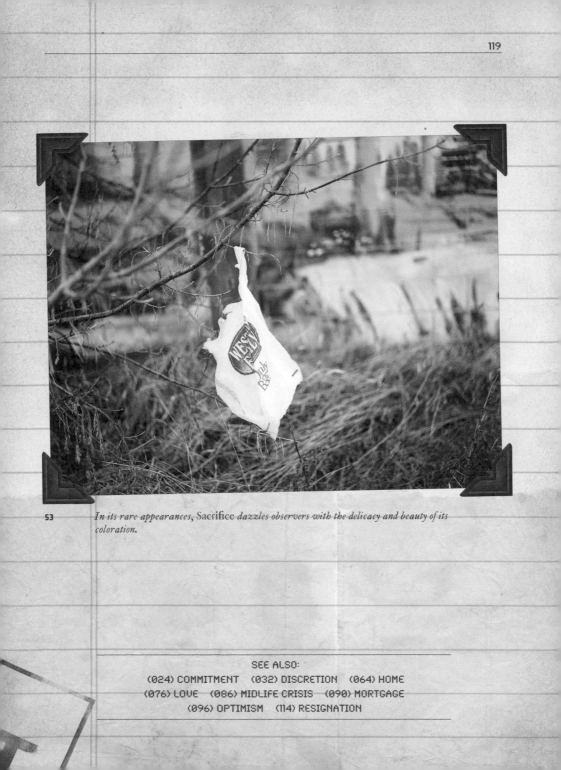

53 *In its rare appearances, Sacrifice dazzles observers with the delicacy and beauty of its coloration.*

SECRET

Lacey's was that she knew. Not immediately, but well before Tommy came to her with the story he'd heard from a, quote, reliable source. She knew as soon as she said it was a lie that it wasn't. Moreover, she knew why Gabe did it, and that she still wouldn't let him go. She kept it hidden, smothered the grenade with her body, until the night he himself confessed it to her, half-undressed on the edge of her childhood bed with its pink dustruffle, with its canopy. "I know," she told him. That more than anything, she knows now, is what sent him running off that night, the night he would end up in the hospital.

54   Secrets *breed rapidly. In concentration, they are the host organisms for* Rumor.

SECURITY

In light of all that's happened to these poor folks in little over a year, you have to be feeling pretty good looking around the dinner table at your own loved ones. Divorce and estrangement have never entered your home, nor has the misery of a prolonged hospitalization. And if death has touched you, well, you've all moved on. You can sit here in the dimmerswitch quiet long after the last sun has fled from the windows and enjoy a meal together, just the three of you. You can gaze on their faces, peaceably chewing, free from all but minor blemishes. Your son has slimmed down, you notice, and your daughter still sports a healthy glow from her cheerleading practice. And if their eyes are a little dark, it's because they worry, too, about the misfortune that can visit good people. After all, you've raised them right, cultivated in them the compassion so missing from the culture these days. Or so you think, until your son opens his mouth.

55   *Security is prized by breeders for its handsome coat and protective disposition. When confined to small spaces, however, the Security has been known to turn on its master.*

SEE ALSO:
(026) CONSENSUS   (030) DEPRESSION   (074) IRONY
(062) HOLIDAY   (092) MYTHOLOGY   (096) OPTIMISM
(126) TANTRUM   (132) UNCERTAINTY

SIBLING RIVALRY

⟡————⟡

Moms say they're supposed to take care of you, but this big brother is just not like that. He's mean. Like when I was in the living room and my mom was listening to her headphones and then my dad asked her if she had something she wanted to tell him and all of a sudden they were fighting, I went to the basement where my brother was. I was in Third Grade and he was in Ninth but he said go away. The lights were off. He was just sitting there. I could just hear his voice over the music, like a monster's in a cave. "I said go away," he said. So I went up to my room to say prayers, but I still remember that night, so anytime anybody tells me how lucky I am to have a big brother, I just think to myself no way. I'm the only one who cares about me. Well, and Alphonse, too, if you count Alphonse.

56   *The* Sibling Rivalry *hunts in groups of two or more. With its tremendous longevity, it may hibernate for years between periods of activity. This* Rivalry, *like species on other continents, tends to lose some of its vitality with age.*

SEE ALSO:
(018) ANGST   (020) BOREDOM   (034) DIVORCE
(036) ENTERTAINMENT   (082) MATURITY   (100) PHASE
(112) RECONCILIATION   (138) YOUTH

TANTRUM

In an obscure way, I knew, it was my fault. If I hadn't told Lacey what I heard about Gabe, they wouldn't have fought. If they hadn't fought, he wouldn't have run out of her room, past my room, where I had been lying high with the lights off, trying to pretend not to exist. It was as though all of that garbage I had told that shrink after my dad died had suddenly and strangely come true. Of course, awareness didn't dawn on me immediately. It waited until the night just before New Year's when I made my mom cry by telling her that if she kept trying to ply us with turkey, to stuff us with ham, to silence us with roast beef, we would all end up like my dad. Walking through the frozen streets of the subdivision after that, I knew that the guilt was going to eat me alive, and from the inside. I knew, all of a sudden, that it would never stop as long as I stayed there in Stony Brook, where I'd already invented my destiny.